Dear Meadow — (MEADOW)

Always have adventures! they
make great stories! I hope
you like Keeno & Ernest!

Always follow your dreams!

Morgan van C

The Adventures of Keeno and Ernest
"The Banana Tree"

By Maggie van Galen

Illustrated by Joanna Lundeen

Outskirts Press, Inc.
Denver, Colorado

The Adventures of Keeno and Ernest
The Banana Tree
All Rights Reserved.
Copyright © 2012 Maggie van Galen
V2.0

Illustrations created by Joanna Lundeen

Outskirts Press, Inc.
http://www.outskirtspress.com

ISBN: 978-1-4327-7982-5

Library of Congress Control Number: 2011919318

Outskirts Press and the "OP" logo are trademarks belonging to Outskirts Press, Inc.

PRINTED IN THE UNITED STATES OF AMERICA

This book is dedicated to my father.
Thanks, Dad, for always telling great stories!

Thank you to my beautiful boys, Luke and Dylan, and to my wonderful husband for always being there for me and encouraging me to see my dream through. I love you higher than the sky and deeper than the deepest ocean!

A special thanks to all of my family and friends, the teachers of my children, and children's friends that have listened to my stories and encouraged me to publish.

Once upon a time, deep in the jungle, there lived two best friends. The first was a very mischievous monkey named Keeno. Keeno was always getting himself into trouble. But thankfully for Keeno, his best friend in the whole world was a wise elephant named Ernest. Ernest was always there for Keeno.

One day while Keeno was swinging on the vines high in the forest canopy he spotted a bright, yellow glow off in the distance. As he moved closer, he saw a giant, yummy, banana tree . . . just on the other side of the river.

"Wow!" said Keeno as his tummy started to rumble. "Look at all of those bananas. I have got to tell Ernest about this!"

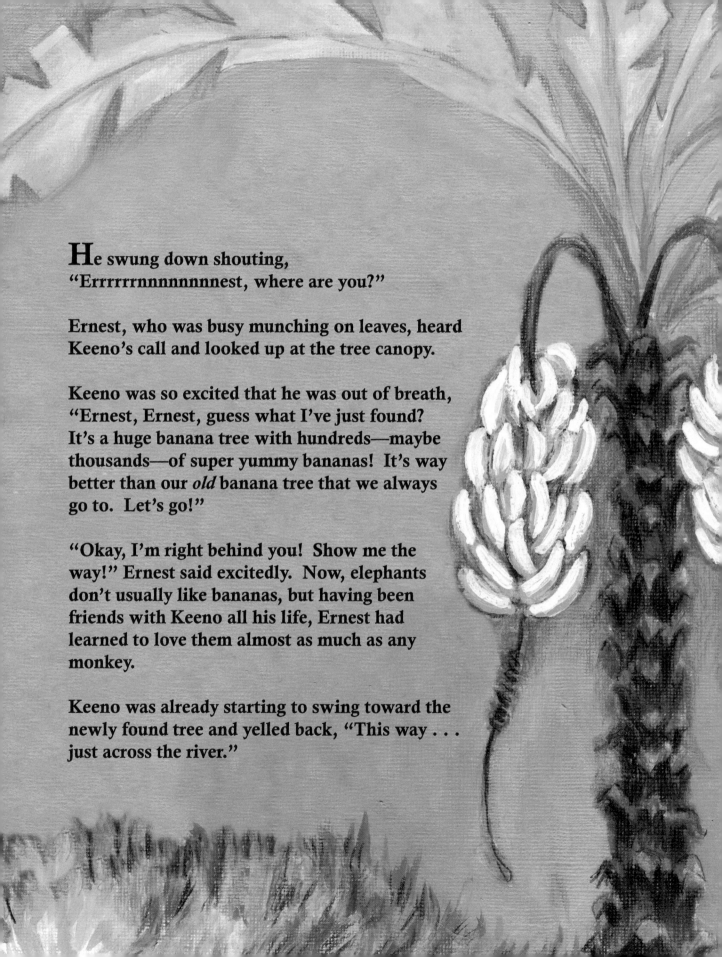

He swung down shouting,
"Errrrrrnnnnnnnnnest, where are you?"

Ernest, who was busy munching on leaves, heard
Keeno's call and looked up at the tree canopy.

Keeno was so excited that he was out of breath,
"Ernest, Ernest, guess what I've just found?
It's a huge banana tree with hundreds—maybe
thousands—of super yummy bananas! It's way
better than our *old* banana tree that we always
go to. Let's go!"

"Okay, I'm right behind you! Show me the
way!" Ernest said excitedly. Now, elephants
don't usually like bananas, but having been
friends with Keeno all his life, Ernest had
learned to love them almost as much as any
monkey.

Keeno was already starting to swing toward the
newly found tree and yelled back, "This way . . .
just across the river."

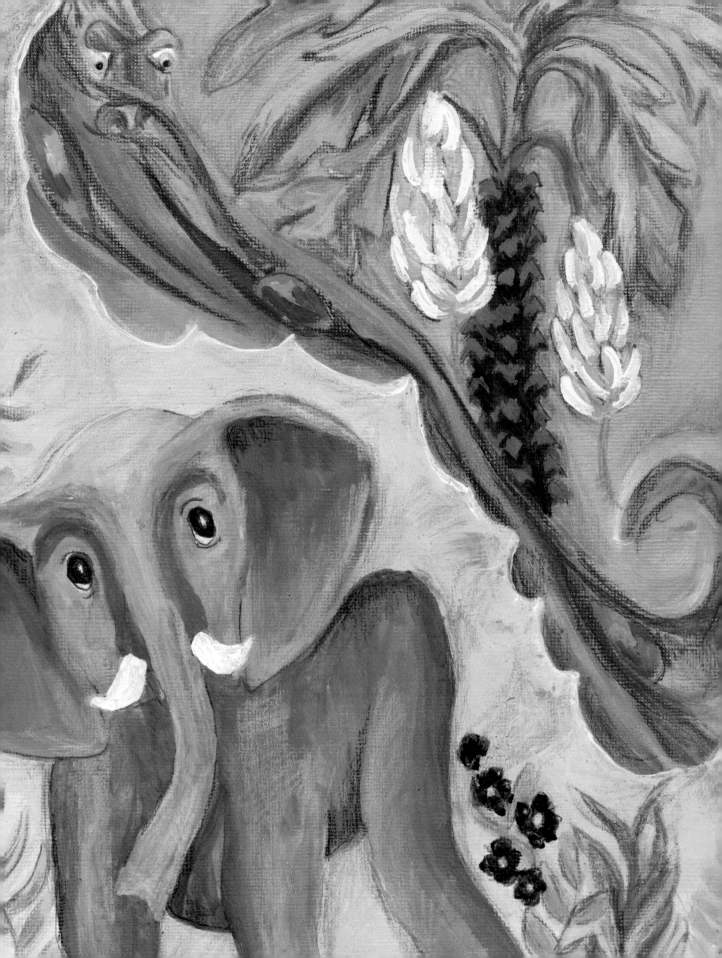

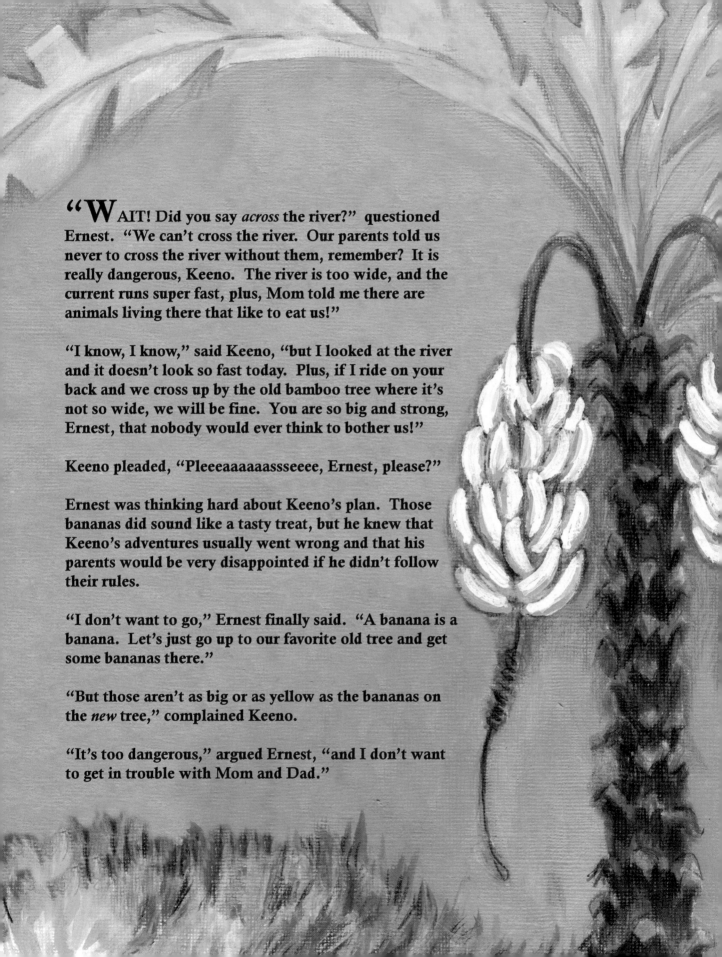

"**W**AIT! Did you say *across* the river?" questioned Ernest. "We can't cross the river. Our parents told us never to cross the river without them, remember? It is really dangerous, Keeno. The river is too wide, and the current runs super fast, plus, Mom told me there are animals living there that like to eat us!"

"I know, I know," said Keeno, "but I looked at the river and it doesn't look so fast today. Plus, if I ride on your back and we cross up by the old bamboo tree where it's not so wide, we will be fine. You are so big and strong, Ernest, that nobody would ever think to bother us!"

Keeno pleaded, "Pleeeaaaaaassseeee, Ernest, please?"

Ernest was thinking hard about Keeno's plan. Those bananas did sound like a tasty treat, but he knew that Keeno's adventures usually went wrong and that his parents would be very disappointed if he didn't follow their rules.

"I don't want to go," Ernest finally said. "A banana is a banana. Let's just go up to our favorite old tree and get some bananas there."

"But those aren't as big or as yellow as the bananas on the *new* tree," complained Keeno.

"It's too dangerous," argued Ernest, "and I don't want to get in trouble with Mom and Dad."

"Okay, fine," Keeno said with a pout on his face. "I guess I'll meet you up at the *old* tree."

Ernest started off toward their favorite old tree, and Keeno swung back up into the forest planning to meet him there. As Keeno got up into the tops of the trees, he saw those bananas across the river again. They were shimmering in the late-morning sun and looked sooooooo delicious!

Suddenly, Keeno had an idea. "I will build a raft out of bamboo and vines, float across the river, grab a bunch of the bananas and surprise Ernest with them. I'll be there and back before he even gets to our old tree. He's going to be so sorry that he missed the adventure!"

It didn't take Keeno long to put together his raft. He put 10 bamboo poles side by side and then tied them together with vines. He grabbed an extra long stick to use as a paddle. Keeno pushed off from the riverbank and slowly started floating toward the other side.

"Ha, this is easy," Keeno said to himself with a smile. The shiny new banana tree was getting closer and closer. He could almost taste them!

As the raft got closer to the middle of the river, a funny thing started to happen. Instead of going across, he started to float *down* the river. He paddled harder, but it didn't make any difference. The current was too strong and began to carry Keeno away.

What am I going to do? thought Keeno.

As Keeno was trying to sort out how he would get himself out of this mess, he heard a dull roaring noise in the distance.

"What's that?" Keeno said aloud. "It can't be the lions. They sleep during the day. It can't be a thunderstorm. There's not a cloud in the sky."

The noise was getting louder and louder as Keeno went further down the river. Keeno was getting worried.

Just then, Keeno and Ernest's friend Toucan Tom flew overhead. His rainbow-colored beak shone brightly in the late-morning sun. Tom looked down and saw Keeno waving frantically at him. Tom swooped down and landed on the raft.

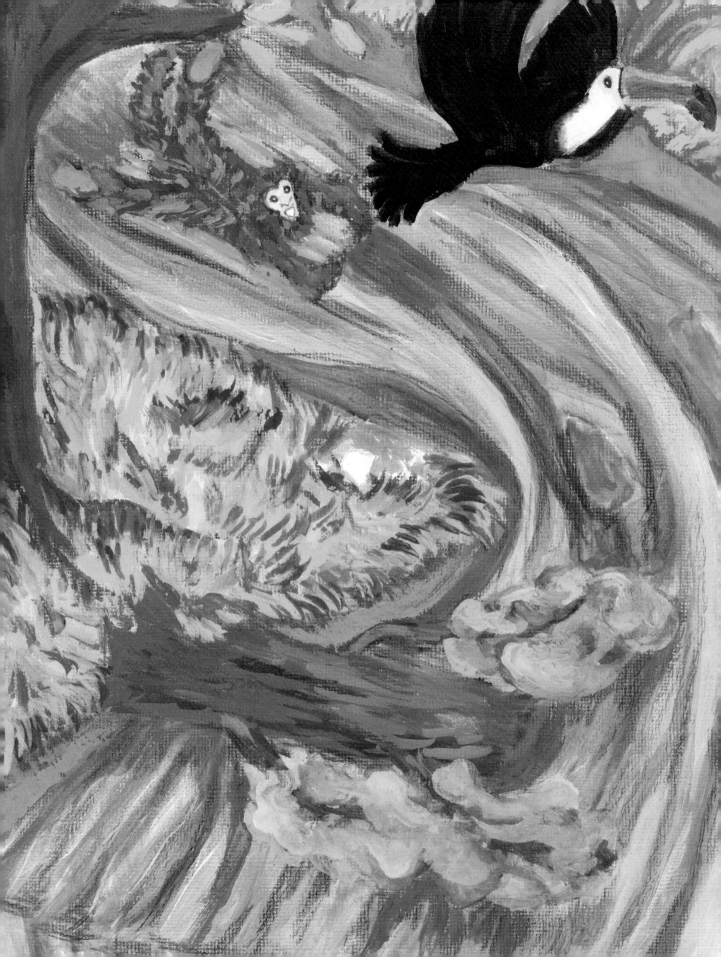

"Nice raft, Keeno," Toucan Tom said. "What are you doing?"

Keeno told him the story of the banana tree, the raft, his plan to surprise Ernest with the new bananas, and the current taking him away. "By the way, Tom," Keeno asked, "what is that loud noise up ahead?"

"That is the waterfall, Keeno," Tom said in a worried voice. "And you are headed straight for it!"

"W . . . w . . . waterfall?" Keeno started to get scared. "Tom, you have to find Ernest! He'll know what to do. He always knows what to do! Quick, he's headed up to the old banana tree. Tell him what's happening and bring him back."

Tom flew off as fast as his wings would carry him.

"HURRY!" shouted Keeno behind him.

It didn't take long for Tom to find Ernest. "Ernest, Ernest," Toucan Tom was yelling as he dove through the forest, weaving in and out of vines and narrowly missing trees.

Ernest looked up in surprise. "What is it, Tom?"

"It's Keeno!" screeched Tom. "He's in trouble on the river!"

"*On* the river?" questioned Ernest.

"Yes, come quick! Hurry!" Tom was almost out of breath. "I'll tell you on the way."

Toucan Tom repeated the story that Keeno had told and explained about the waterfall and how Keeno was only moments away from real danger.

"You have to do something, Ernest," said Tom with a fearful look in his eye.

Ernest was already running at top speed, slaloming trees and trampling bushes. He was thinking and planning as he went.

As they neared the riverbank, he could see Keeno drifting toward the waterfall. He was waving his arms and yelling, "Help! Oh, Ernest, help me please!"

"Don't worry, Keeno," Ernest yelled back. "I'll save you!"

Ernest ran up ahead to look at the waterfall and plan his rescue. He noticed that just before the falls the river narrowed and on the opposite side, a tree had toppled over and stuck straight out. Ernest devised the rescue plan. He would wade out into the river and stretch his trunk as far as he could, and Tom would fly over to the dead tree to mark it. Keeno could then jump to either side. It was his only chance.

Ernest told Tom the plan. Tom flew out to the raft to explain it to Keeno. Keeno was still scared, but he knew that Ernest was his best friend and had never let him down before.

As his raft rounded the last bend in the river, Keeno could see Ernest out in the river, only his head and trunk above the water. Toucan Tom was perched on the tip of the tree that reached out from the other side. Keeno began to paddle as hard and fast as he could.

He was trying to aim for Ernest, and much to his delight, the raft was going in the right direction. *I'm going to be saved*, thought Keeno delightedly.

Keeno was within arm's reach of Ernest when suddenly, the raft spun around from a change in the current. Keeno almost lost his balance, but thanks to his good jumping, he leapt toward Ernest and just managed to wrap around his trunk. The raft shot out from under him and went over the waterfall. The three friends watched as the raft broke up into little pieces.

Keeno was shaking with fright . . . and relief. Ernest slowly backed out of the river and up onto the bank. He lowered his trunk to the ground, but Keeno wouldn't let go.

"I'm soooooooooooo sorry, Ernest," Keeno cried. "Thank you for saving me."

"Of course you are welcome, Keeno," Ernest said. "I'm just glad you are all right and didn't get hurt. But you should never have tried to cross the river. There are reasons our parents don't let us. I'd say this is a pretty good reason, wouldn't you?"

"I know," said Keeno, still shaken. "You are my best friend in the whole jungle, Ernest, and I promise not to get into any more trouble."

Ernest laughed. "Well, I doubt that, but you are my best friend too, and I will always be there to get you out of trouble! Now, let's go home and tell your parents what happened."

Before heading home, the two friends decided to head up to their favorite old banana tree and bring a bunch of yummy bananas home to Keeno's mom. She makes the best banana cream pie anywhere and maybe, just maybe, it would make telling her what had happened . . . a little easier!

CPSIA information can be obtained
at www.ICGtesting.com
Printed in the USA
262911LV00001B

* 9 7 8 1 4 3 2 7 7 9 8 2 5 *